3 3052 09370 3173

D0382466

A FRIEND FOR
GROWL BEAR

A Friend for Growl Bear   Text copyright © 1999 by Sharon A. Riley   Adapted from the text of *Growl Bear* by Margot Austin
Copyright © 1951, copyright renewed 1979   Illustrations copyright © 1999 by David McPhail   Printed in the U.S.A. All rights reserved.
http://www.harperchildrens.com

Library of Congress Cataloging-in-Publication Data   Austin, Margot.   A friend for Growl Bear / by Margot Austin ; illustrated by David
McPhail.   p.   cm.   Summary: None of the animals in the forest will play with a little bear because he is always growling—until they
come to understand that he only growls because he has not learned to talk yet.   ISBN 0-06-027802-1   [1. Bears—Fiction.   2. Animals—
Fiction.   3. Oral communication—Fiction.]   I. McPhail, David, ill.   II. Title.   PZ7.A925Gr 1999   97-34347   [E]—dc21   CIP   AC
Typography by Al Cetta   1 2 3 4 5 6 7 8 9 10   ❖   First Edition

To Nathan and his mom and dad
—D.M.

A FRIEND FOR
GROWL BEAR

BY MARGOT AUSTIN · ILLUSTRATED BY DAVID McPHAIL

HARPERCOLLINSPUBLISHERS

PUBLIC LIBRARY
FORT COLLINS, COLORADO

Once there was a very little bear named Growl Bear,
who lived with his mother in a hollow tree in a
beautiful green wood.

Growl Bear's mother loved him very much. But all the other animals thought Growl Bear was mean, because he always growled, "Gr-r-r-r-r-r!" They were all afraid that Growl Bear would bite them!

So little Growl Bear had no one to play with at all. And he felt very sad.

Then one day Growl Bear went to the oak tree where wise Old Owl lived. Maybe Old Owl could help him make friends.

So he knocked on Old Owl's door, and Old Owl
said, "Who-o-o's there?"

"Gr-r-r-r," Growl Bear said.

"Gr-r-r-r indeed!" said Old Owl. "You can't scare
me. You're too little."

"Gr-r-r-r!" said Growl Bear even louder.

"Just for that extra gr-r-r-r," scowled Old Owl,
"I'll tell everyone that they needn't be afraid of you
anymore. Why, you're so little that you haven't any
teeth! Now go away!" And Old Owl shut the door.

Growl Bear was very happy because Old Owl was going to tell everyone not to be afraid of him anymore. So the next day, bright and early, Growl Bear trotted through the wood to look for his new friends.

First he saw Rabbit.

"Gr-r-r!" said Growl Bear.

"Gr-r-r yourself," said Rabbit. "Old Owl told me you can't bite, and I'm not afraid of you anymore!"

And Rabbit pushed Growl Bear into the brook. *Splas-s-h!*

Growl Bear waded out of the brook and trotted along till he came upon Squirrel.

"Gr-r-r-r," said Growl Bear.

"Go away," said Squirrel. "Old Owl told me you haven't any teeth, and I'm not afraid of you anymore!" And he hit Growl Bear on the nose with a chestnut. *Wha-a-ack!*

Then Growl Bear thought that maybe Mouse
would play with him. So he sat on a log and
wriggled his ears. But Mouse did not come.

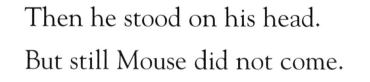

Then he stood on his head.
But still Mouse did not come.

Finally he climbed onto a tree limb
and hung upside down.

And Mouse, who was very curious, came!

"Gr-r-r," said Growl Bear.

Cra-a-ack! The limb broke, and
down came poor Growl Bear.

"Serves you right!" squeaked Mouse,
scampering away.

Then Growl Bear thought that maybe
the songbirds would play with him. So he climbed
the nearest tree.

"Gr-r-r," he said.

"Gr-r-r yourself," sang the songbirds, and they flew round Growl Bear's head so fast that he got dizzy and down he tumbled—*Bump! Thump! Thud!*

Poor little Growl Bear was sore all over, and he
felt very sad. So he went back to the oak tree where
Old Owl lived and knocked on Old Owl's door.

"Gr-r-r-r," said Growl Bear when Old Owl popped out his head.

"I already told you that you can't scare me," hooted Old Owl. "And I told you to go away." And he slammed the door in Growl Bear's face.

"Gr-r-r," said poor little Growl Bear, and he began to cry.

Just then Old Owl opened his door a crack and said, "I've been thinking. . . ."

"Gr-r?" said Growl Bear, wiping his eyes.

"I've been thinking," said Old Owl, opening the door a little more, "that maybe you're not trying to scare anyone after all."

"Gr-r-r!" said Growl Bear, sitting up straight. "Bother!" hooted Old Owl, opening his door wide and peering hard at Growl Bear. "I see it all now! You just can't say anything but 'Gr-r-r!'"

And the next day, before Growl Bear was even wide awake, there in his front yard were all his friends and Old Owl, too.

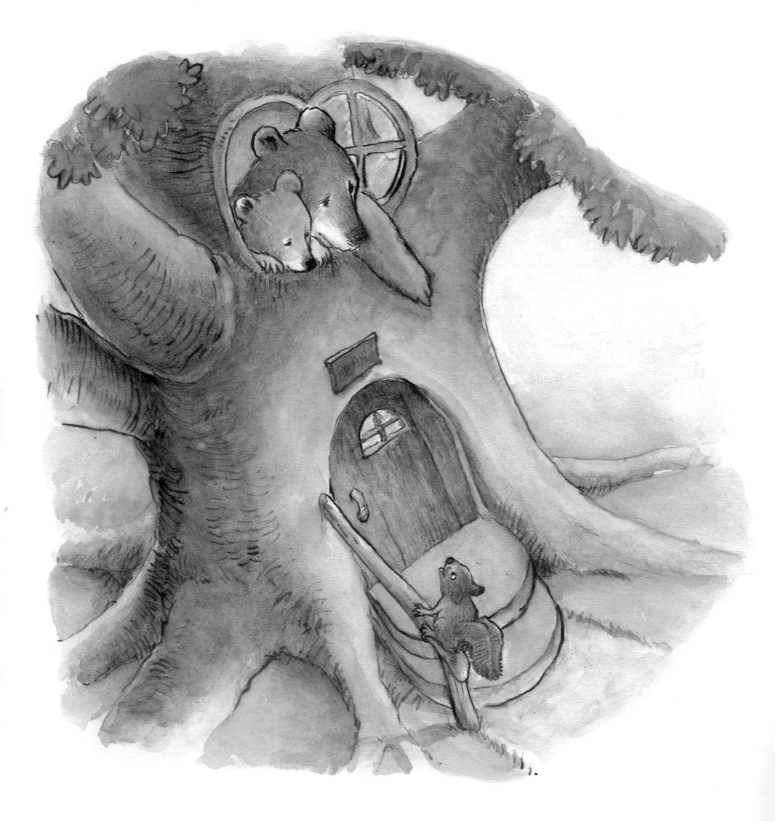

"Er-r ahem," said Old Owl, clearing his throat. "I've told everyone that you aren't trying to scare them at all.

"I told them," said Old Owl, "that you're just so very little that you haven't learned to talk yet!"

And with a happy smile, Growl Bear said, "G-r-r-r."

And from then on,
Growl Bear's friends were always waiting
for him to come out and play.